To Mike
Thank you for your
continued support
Best Wishes
Gemma xx

Red Light Romance

By

Gemma Owen-Kendall

Dedication

To my friend I once knew, this book is dedicated to you.

Author's Introduction about Red Light Romance

Back in August 2018 I visited the city of Amsterdam for a weekend break away, I'd heard many stories of those who have visited this place. Often the stories are about walking through the Red Light District, I won't mention any names. My partner John had visited the city twice already so I was determined that we would go together for a weekend away. As he knew the place so well, he definitely was the right person to take me round the sites and tourist attractions. When we landed at Schipol airport, we tried to locate the relevant public transport as well as checking on John's phone to decide where to head to first once we arrived in the city. Scrolling through google maps, we noticed that the canal was multi-coloured, very similar to the colours of the rainbow. We couldn't understand at that moment why there was a rainbow around the canal.

Once we stepped off the shuttle bus by the Museums and headed to find De Vier Pilaren, a pancake house John had gone to on one of his previous visits. We noticed all the banners up stating Pride, it then clicked we had come on the weekend of Amsterdam's LGBTQ+ Pride weekend. This turned out to be a very fun filled and atmospheric time away in Amsterdam, one that I still to this day remember very well.

My story of Red Light Romance is completely fictional and came to me whilst we were on the train back to Schipol airport, what if one of those girls on the red light district fell in love with a secret agent and needed to be rescued. This is how my story was born.

<u>Trigger Warnings:</u>

Drug Abuse

Rape

Suicide

Violence

Sex

Prologue:Lucy

Gazing around this windowless room that feels like a prison cell, I've been taken in for questioning by the ministry of defence. Although I appreciate to be back in England finally, it's all for the wrong reasons. Standing before me are two agents dressed suited and booted with straight looks upon their faces. They've handcuffed me to the chair, I'm not sure what relevance this will have as I'm not a criminal, I know I've not done anything wrong. I should be put into the witness protection programme after what I've been through. I reflect over the past six months of my life. This is my story of the girl who worked in Amsterdam, not by choice but to help those I love dearly and to hope that I will be rescued someday......

Chapter One - Sophie

My dearest cousin Lucy,

He found me, he tracked me down on facebook and found me here. I can't even say or write his name on my final letter to you as I can't bear to think his name. Please forgive me but I can't fight this anymore, he has done it again what he did to me when I was fourteen only this time, he has left me a present to help me end my pain. I am truly so sorry, look after Maria for me just like I know she will look after you. The demons inside me have won and now it is time to set them free.

I love you both so very much.

Sophie

Xxxx

To my love Maria,

I'm truly sorry but I have to leave you, leave this cruel world. You know who has found me, he's been stalking me through facebook and tracked me down to Amsterdam. Please forgive me on my decision, I can't fight this pain anymore and I feel like there is no escaping him. Please take good care of Sophie for me. I've deeply let her down and I know she is going to need you.

I love you with all my heart and soul. This is just a temporary goodbye for now until one day where we will be reunited in spirit.

Sophie

xxxxxxxxxxxxx

Chapter Two - Lucy

Red lights are the colour over my window as I gaze out onto the busy bricked street; there are many people from all walks of life heading past my window every day. I stand here looking out at everyone most days apart from Mondays as I like to give myself a full day off. It gives me a chance to browse round the area without having to worry about dashing back to my red light window. It also allows me to admire the smells of Dutch pancakes and Marijuana in the air. I do the long walk from my working window that I pay 85 euro a night to rent and head over to the museums. My favourite pancake restaurant "De Vier Pilaren" is located right by the Vincent Van Gogh museum, I need to have this one day to myself to be a normal person in this beautiful place called Amsterdam.

Today is a Monday so of course my day off, I sit in the same corner in my favourite pancake restaurant and my choice of the day is for my pancake to be served with lemon curd. The owner is a friendly native lady reaching close to retirement age but she is always welcoming and so kind to me. The smell of cooking batter lingers in the air filling my nostrils with the sweet smells of sugar and syrup. The same table I often sit at has the engravings of wear and tear along the wooden surface.

Six months ago I came out to Amsterdam to visit my cousin who lived over here. I'd only intended to stay for a week but due to unforeseen circumstances I had been made to believe I needed to earn a visa to continue my life out here and that eventually I would have to fork out for one within a year. Of course nevertheless this was the case due to Brexit in January 2021. I'd originally came out here as a break away from my life in England and at the age of twenty one I had experienced my first and only heartache. Dean was the guy I loved so much and after three years of us being together, he suddenly ended our relationship. He was in the army so of course it was tough trying to make things work for us, it was hard not to be able to see each other for months on end. The day he called it off would've been perfect for us, we had spent the weekend away in London at a hotel called the Ruebans located near Buckingham Palace. As we got to kings' cross station to sit in Starbucks to have a goodbye coffee before we parted ways, he announced that a huge job offer came up in the army, which he couldn't turn down so had to make the decision to end things with me. He didn't mention what it was, but he had to end things with me because of this new position, I ran off crying and caught the next train home. I just didn't want to say goodbye and I was too upset to wish him good luck for the future. There was the odd text message I received from him asking if I was ok, that he was very sorry but it took me about a month to finally respond back to him, as well as wish him luck on his new job role. I had also mentioned to him I was going to visit my cousin in Amsterdam as a breather to clear my head. I can remember the last message I got from Dean was a joke about me ending up staying in the city and working down the red light district, of course this joke ended up being true but was not overly my choice.

I'd only been in Amsterdam for two days when I found my cousin Sophie on her work bed with a needle in her arm. Sophie was one of the popular prostitutes along the red light district, very beautiful but sadly had a dark side to her. Sophie had a drug problem but I didn't realise how bad it was until that morning I found her cold lifeless body. Unfortunately she had got into some debt with the local drug gangs and she was massively behind on her rent.

At the time I didn't feel like I had much left to live for so I made the decision to take over from Sophie and work as a prostitute. Only recently I'd cleared off Sophie's debts. *Thank you oh kind Kandi* were the last words I got from the drug lord of Amsterdam, Kandi was my work name but my actual name is Lucy. I didn't want anyone knowing my real name and most of the time, I kept myself to myself. Life in Amsterdam wasn't too bad as everyone is pretty laid back but that could be down to the weed. Even if you didn't smoke the stuff, the smell and the fumes in the air was enough to mellow you out.

I'm often stopped in the streets especially by previous clients, asking if I'm the girl who works on the red light district or if I'm the girl they spend an hour in bed with. I just smile and carry on walking away, I have only had one client who has been obsessed with me, his name is Chris. He comes over to Amsterdam every couple of months and straight away he looks for me, since I have been living out in Amsterdam I've gotten to know little things about him. I know he is also from England and is about ten years older than me. Chris runs a business over in Amsterdam so he comes across on a regular basis, he calls me his 'favourite girl' and if I'm not available, he would wait around nearby until I'm free for him.

Chris always booked me up for a night, he would pay me at least five hundred euros so I was only with him. I often wondered what his business over here in Amsterdam was but I never asked, the least I know about him the better and it was best I never got attached to my clients as I could not be doing with any complications. But I did have this gut feeling Chris wanted me all to himself, perhaps more than just one of my clients.

On my day off today, who did I bump into, of course, It was Chris, he never seemed to have a girlfriend. He was quite an attractive guy and had a well-built physique so he did take good care of himself, but for some reason he was never in a relationship.

"Kandi, it is so lovely to see you babe."

He always said the same phrase to me in his husky voice whenever I saw him. It was nice to have attention from a regular guy, but I could never get over Dean at the moment. My heart as well as my feelings still longed for him and often wishing he would appear in this beautiful city to come and find me.

"Nice to see you again Chris, away on business again?" He flirted and winked towards me.

"Sure am, and of course make some time for my favourite girl." I just smiled but inside I wanted to walk away from him, I sort of had grown attached to him deep down, but he creeped me out as well.

"On a day off today?" he asked.

"Yes, I am indeed."

"Well do you fancy some over time tonight and joining me in my hotel room?"

Every time on my day off he would ask me this same question, it was Sophie's policy to never go with a client to a hotel room and as I took over from her, I would always honour her rules and regulations to the working girl's life on the red light district.

"Thank you, Chris, although the extra money would be lovely but I am indeed having a well needed day off."

"You know where I will be staying if you change your mind."

"Yes, I do, take care Chris. As always it is nice to see you."

Before I could walk off, he grabbed hold of my hand, his hands were twice the size of mine and pulled me in towards him, perching his lips onto mine.

"Something for you to remember me by until I see you tomorrow." He said to me in his flirty husky voice. I gave him a shattered smile, I just hoped no one I knew saw this especially the other girls who worked on the same block as me. He gently released his fingers from my left hand.

"Goodbye Chris" I hurried away from him as quickly as I could and headed to my rented room. As I wasn't working tonight I kept my red curtains shut but that never stopped the tourists knocking on my glassed window. I kicked off my shoes and slumped into my dressing table chair, I wished often that Chris would leave me alone but as he pays for my time so generously, I just had to deal with it. Firing up my laptop I login into facebook to check in with my family, as soon as my profile is active my chat springs up an instant message.

Chapter Three - Lucy

In a quick glance seeing who it was from, my heart skipped a beat. The name clearly shows it is Dean and I think back to that moment in Kings Cross station again when he ended things with me. The heartache was just too unbearable, Dean was five years older than me, and we had met at a college open day. He was there with a couple of his fellow army reserves trying to get some of the college graduates to sign up for the army. I had noticed him as soon as I walked into the sports hall, he was tall with a well-toned physique and chocolate brown hair. His grin was so friendly and charming, I also spotted the dimple on his right cheek complimenting his smile. At the time I had Sophie with me and of course I instantly shared my girl crush with her about the soldier boy.

"Go on girl, go speak to him." Urged Sophie whilst nudging me on the ribs.

"Eeek I can't, I am just too damn nervous to approach him." I turned my back from his direction so that I gave Sophie my full focus and to try not get his attention.

"Look Sophie, you know what I'm like when it comes to guys."

"Well maybe you should stop being so afraid and just go for it." I knew Sophie was right, it was so true word for word. Although I was eighteen years old, I was too scared to approach any guy I took a liking to because I was never confident about myself back then.

"I.. I just can't."

"Oh, Lucy don't miss this opportunity to finally approach a guy."

"Well, he probably isn't even interested in me anyway."

"Now is your chance to ask him as he is walking straight towards us."

As soon as I heard her say those words my heart started beating faster and then I wondered if he took a liking towards Sophie. My cousin was so beautiful, her long naturally straight brown hair was just perfect, and she had an amazing toned physique from all the spinning classes we attended together. Everywhere we went together guys would always stop and stare at Sophie.

"Come on Sophie he is probably coming over to speak to you anyway."

I felt a soft fingertip tap my right shoulder; he had walked over to us but yet he wanted my attention. Gazing round to him I couldn't help but just stare at his smile, his teeth were so perfectly white. Sophie politely walked off to give us both chance to talk, also for me to finally chat to a guy without her helping me out. We exchanged numbers and that I hoped we would meet up when he was next back home. I had received a text message from him later that day, I was already looking forward to having the opportunity to see Dean. Now and again, I had messages from him, mostly just trying to get to know him. He had gone to the same college I went to and was really understanding about our little age gap. A week before the day we'd arranged our date, we had the conversation about sex. At the time I was still very unexperienced with having sex with someone, I'd only slept with one person when I was sixteen, but Dean seemed happy to take things slow with me. I was nervous admitting to him how unexperienced I was in the bedroom department, but this had made Dean more interested in me, he wanted to be the one to show me how to pleasure a man.

The first date finally came round; Dean was staying over at a local hotel, Kenwick Park, that was an old Georgian Style house that'd been converted. He had made a reservation for us at the hotel's restaurant which was quite classy for a first date. All day I spent getting ready; Sophie had helped me pick out a nice dress. It was a bit short for my liking, but she pressured me into wearing a pair of six inched heels. I could only just about walk in them but now, I wear these types of heels for work.

Sophie was kind enough to drop me off at the hotel, as a gentlemen Dean was standing by the entrance waiting for me to arrive. The next day I would be returning Sophie the favour by dropping her off at the airport where she would be starting her new adventure in Amsterdam.

Dean looked so handsome; he had really made an effort with his neatly ironed shirt and trousers. He'd folded back his sleeves and the top couple of buttons on his shirt were not fastened up. He had slightly spiked up his hazel brown hair and he still looked just as gorgeous compared to our first time we met, only now he was out of his military uniform.

Over dinner we talked and laughed, I got to learn so much about Dean and how kind he really is. We even had some mutual friends with him being round the same area as me, but we'd never crossed paths. He had joined the army as soon as he left school at sixteen and at the age of twenty-three, he'd ranked up to corporal. Eventually after the three years we had been together he became a sergeant which was a huge achievement for him to gain this rank at the age of twenty-six. He ended things with me not long after he got this promotion.

The meal was lovely, but the company was just the best. I had developed some strong feelings towards Dean in the space of a couple of hours, but I had the sensation of butterflies in my tummy. I was worried that he may not have the same feelings towards me but also, I might have drunk one too many pink gins throughout the evening.

"Fancy joining me for a drink in my room?" the words that I had been dreading but also excited to hear and without thinking I replied with "Yes."

Dean requested our meal to be charged to his room, that he would settle on his departure and also ordered for some drinks to be bought up to his room. The hotel room he was staying in was one of the nicest of hotel rooms I'd seen, it had a king sized bed, flat screen, an en-suite with a hydro bath that was large enough for two people to comfortably lay in. I sat down on the corner of the king sized bed not knowing what was going to happen next. Dean un-buttoned his shirt revealing part of his well-toned torso, I couldn't help but stare at him because he was just so amazingly good looking. My gaze was interrupted by a knock on the door, our drinks had arrived. Dean quickly did up a couple of the buttons on his shirt and answered the door, the night porter greeted Dean and entered the room with a bottle of champagne on ice. I had only ever tried champagne once and that was a glass at a relative's wedding reception when I was sixteen.

The night porter must've guessed what was about to happen next as he didn't hang around for very long, Dean had told him that he would open and serve our own drinks. Dean poured a glass full into the first flute and handed it straight over to me. I took a sip and felt the bubbles go straight to my head, Dean had to remove the flute from my hand as I nearly toppled all over the bed and spilt the champagne everywhere.

"Lucy do you not drink much?" was all he asked me, I had a couple of glasses of pink gin with my meal but I didn't think I'd drunk enough to become tipsy. He sat next to me and held my hand in his for a moment then next of all he placed his lips onto mine. He kissed me so passionately and tenderly, those butterflies in my stomach had gone into overdrive as the kiss was so incredible. Dean moved his hands to my back and began to unzip my dress, this was the first time anyone from the opposite sex had seen me in just my lingerie.

"Wow you have such an incredible body." He whispered to me huskily. I laid down on the bed whilst he removed his shirt revealing his well-toned physique. He perched his shirtless body above me and kissed me passionately once again, I was so ready for him to just to take me now and thrust himself onto me.

"Are you sure you are ready?" he whispered to me gently and smoothly.

"Yes" I answered back to him nervously.

He reached for his right pocket to take out a condom; my first time with Dean was so incredible and was a night I would never forget. However as I was about to climax he pulled out, how dare he tease me in this way, I think from my first encounter with him made me pine for him still.

Now hearing from him again after a few months was not what I was expecting, he wrote 'Hey how's tricks?' and before I processed the words I was instantly responding back to him. I missed him so much and still loved him so dearly. I wished I knew what his current mission in the army was and wondered if he still loved me like I did for him. That evening we chatted online for ages, he asked me questions like 'Where I was and where my job is?' I could not tell him the truth, so I lied and made out I was in London working for an entertainment company. I sort of was ashamed of myself on my current path I was in. I still loved him very much for sure and could not let him know where I was. However things would soon change between us forever.

Chapter Four - Lucy

A few nights later after my last conversation with Dean, I was doing my usual shift in my rented room. This particular night I put on my sexiest outfit, it was black and only just covered parts of my chest and to try bringing in some customers, I thought I would curl parts of my hair gazing into my mirror. Then next of all my regular client Chris came knocking at my glassed door and as I approached to open it and let him inside, a familiar face caught the corner of my eye. Then both of my eyes moved in the direction where I saw him, Dean. He was with a couple of other guys about his age, and they were all looking in my direction. A sickening feeling arose from my stomach up to my throat. I had lied to the man I love and now he had caught me out, even worse it was the moment where I was chatting to Chris and greeting him into my rented room. The look on Dean's face was blank like he either wasn't expecting to see me or he wasn't hoping I would be in this situation. I grabbed hold of Chris and quickly shut the door behind him then pulled the curtains across so Dean couldn't see any more of me.

"Someone happy to see me ay." Chris said huskily with slight excitement in his tone of voice.

"I…erm.. just didn't want to waste any of your time."

That was the first ridiculous excuse I could come up with for him that came to my head, but he hadn't acknowledged much of what I had just said as he was straight into his wallet going through his Euros. As usual it was the full amount for him to book me up for the rest of the night. Although I spent the night with Chris, I just could not get over seeing Dean again, that moment seeing him was just playing over and over in my head. Chris had noticed I seemed a little distracted tonight, but I managed to shrug it off and I just mentioned I was hoping to go back to England to visit my family as I did miss them a lot. Not even they knew I was working along the red light district. My little sob story had earned me an extra tip from Chris, so he must've felt a bit sorry for me.

The next morning was a glorious sunny day, it was round about eleven when Chris decided he would exit my room. I saw him out and as always, he gave me a kiss on the cheek. I watched him walk away, eyeing him up when at that moment Dean approached me, I hadn't noticed him and I was not dressed properly as I only had a bed sheet wrapped round me. Dean hadn't seen me like this in over six months, I felt quite ashamed and shy seeing him again. I tried to quickly shut the door but he overpowered me and let himself in, the linger in the air of my room was not pleasant as I needed to freshen it up. He made sure the curtains were shut and the door was locked.

"So how long have you been working as a…" he couldn't bring himself to say the word. I noticed the look of disappointment in his face but then how dare he be so ashamed of me doing what I do for work.

"Go on then, say it." I tried to force the words out of his mouth, but he just continued his look of disappointment towards me.

"Let me explain then why I do what I do for work." I took a deep breath; I hadn't cried over my cousin for a few months but now I could feel all the raw emotions come flooding back to me. I told him everything on Sophie about what she did to herself, that I felt obliged to clear up her mess and I that I was pretty much stuck like this for the time being. The tears then came flooding out after all the hurt and pain I had kept locked up for some time.

"Oh Lucy, I hadn't realised. I am so sorry."

"Oh, save your sympathy, it's not like you have been there for me through all of this."

Through my teary eyes I could see the look of disappointment change to guilt, he left me heartbroken, so it was a slight relief to finally pour all my hurt onto him. I needed to know where he had been these past six months, but it angered me to think if he had been with anyone else. I longed for a shower as well wanting to clear off the sweat and lust from spending the night with Chris.

"So, who was that guy then?" he sounded jealous

"None of your business really, just a client."

"He came across more than just a client to me." He still sounded very jealous.

"He is a regular client; I don't mix work with my private life." I don't know why I made him want to feel relieved I was not involved with anyone else.

"So, I guess I have nothing to worry about trying to get you back?"

He wanted me back. The words I had longed to hear for too long, I couldn't focus straight as there was no way I could forgive him just yet.

"I need a shower before I continue this conversation with you." He took out a hotel room key and handed it straight over to me.

"I don't sleep with clients in their hotel rooms."

"I am not requesting that, I just thought you could take a shower back at the hotel I am staying at. It is much nicer…"

He was right about a nicer shower as my rented room didn't really have the best facilities to live in. They were mainly done up to sleep with clients and for us working ladies to use as and when. But firstly, I grabbed my cleaning products as I needed to sort out my room ready for tonight. Dean offered to help but I assured him I was fine and suggested he wait for me outside; I couldn't let him see a bin full of used condoms and cum stained sheets. I shouldn't have really let him into my rented room but luckily no one had seen. The city is normally pretty quiet in the mornings until after midday. Once I had cleaned up to my satisfactory standards, I grabbed my clothes I'd worn the day before my shift started, denim short skirt with a white gypsy style top and white sandals. I just tied my hair up in a ponytail so that it was off my face, it felt like straw from the amount of hair spray I had put on it last night, I was ready to go. I securely locked up my room with my notice of closed / Gesloten on show to try keep the punters away.

We walked by the canal as it was such a gorgeous day in August and the streets were getting ready for pride weekend which was about to happen any day now. This particular event is one of the most popular events of Amsterdam, just after Kings Day that happens in April. Instead of the city just turning orange, it had colours of the rainbow, red, orange, tallow, green, blue and purple. I'd never been in Amsterdam during the pride event, but I was already liking what I saw. There had been the odd female client from time to time, but I am happy to do whatever when it comes to my current job.

The boats along the canal floated gracefully on the water surface, this was something I had never done as of yet, to go on a boat ride through the city. But I was determined to make this happen someday, but I had the fear of always being alone. Working six out of seven days a week was often too much for me. I daydreamed of being free from this life but there was nothing else for me to do until I built up enough savings. Paying off Sophie's debts nearly bankrupted me, if it hadn't been for Chris paying me the rates he does, I don't think I would ever have paid off those drug dealers. Dean noticed I was gazing along the canal in a world of my own. He obviously was talking to me, and I wasn't paying attention to what he was saying, he took a glance to see what I was looking at.

"Lucy, Earth to Lucy." He nudged me in the ribs.

"Woah, Sorry." I awoke from my daydream, I was not ready to share the whole sad story on how I longed to be rescued, but I was determined to one day free myself. Dean playfully picked me up and pretended to chuck me into the canal, I let out a joyful scream, laughing but yelling 'please put me down' although I knew he wouldn't really throw me in, but it was great to be having a little giggle for a change with a familiar face. As he gently put me back to my feet I gazed up into his eyes, those beautiful eyes again that I hadn't seen since the last moment we had in kings cross station. Damn it I still love him so much; he just makes me go so weak and I have no control of myself. We approached his hotel, The Radisson Blu on Rusland right in the centre of Amsterdam. There was no way I could afford to stay in this hotel.

"Is this where you are staying?"

Dean just smiled, showing off those dimples and nodded at me to acknowledge this is where he was currently staying, he must be on a good salary with his promotion. The hotel reception was so light and open, there was a glimpse of how the other half live. I felt too under dressed to be standing in a place like this.

We headed to his hotel room, number 201, the whole room was twice the size of my rented working room. There was a king sized bed, a desk area where Dean's Apple mac was on charge with a few files neatly stacked. He showed me to the bathroom which was also larger than my rented room, he left me to get sorted, even leaving the hotel room. It was so nice to be out and about having a taster of what it is like to have a life instead of working all the time and just scraping through each week on my current nightly earnings.

By the time I had my shower Dean returned with some retail shopping bags from Topshop, I must've been in the shower for quite some time as he had plenty of time to walk there and back here with his purchases.

"I thought you could do with some new clothes. I am hoping I have remembered your size, but you have lost some weight since I last saw you. Not like there was anything bad with your weight previously."

Towel wrapped tightly round myself I rummaged through the plastic carrier bags on the few items of ladies' clothes he had purchased for me. I was pretty impressed with the choice of clothing and lingerie.

"Thank you so much but don't expect sex out of me for free." His smile immediately dropped, perhaps that was quite cruel of me to think he would want that in return. Obviously, my job had made me get the impression that every bloke in Amsterdam just wanted to have sex with me.

"Sorry, I shouldn't have said that. I guess being out here for a while has made me believe that is just what everyone wants from me." I put a comforting hand on his right shoulder, he immediately placed his left hand over mine. I felt the muscles under his clothes, he always liked to work out even when we were together.

"This has been hard for me to see you out here, working as you are." I saw the hurt in his eyes, and I just wished for that moment back at Kings Cross to happen again but to have been a happy time and for us to still be together.

"It is hard on me to see you again; I was devastated that you ended things with me especially after a wonderful weekend away.

"I wish I could tell you why I had to end things with you. I haven't been with anyone else since you." What I had been dreading never happened or so he says. I was the last woman he laid with.

"I do deserve an answer as to why you did." I needed to know as I may finally have a bit of closure towards Dean and gradually forgive him for breaking my heart.

"It's Friday, I have no plans with the guys tonight so I was wondering will you let me take you out for dinner?"

"I would love that, but I need to work tonight."

"Is there anything I can say or do to make you change your mind?"

"If I didn't need the money to save up and go back to England, I would be staying shut tonight."

Checking the time on my mobile phone I knew I had to head back soon and start to get ready for my window shift. I gathered up my new clothes, did my hair and make-up in Dean's hotel room then made a dash for it to my rented room. It was nearly 4pm by the time I got back so I had been away for a good few hours. The other working girls were already in their windows trying to get the attention of passers-by. I quickly put my room into working order, I was so glad I had cleaned up this morning after last night. Searching through my lingerie drawers I chose a black and purple corset with jasmine black crotch-less panties with fishnet stockings. I was feeling quite turned on from seeing Dean today. After I was ready and dressed for work, I opened my curtains and switched on the red light. The punters then started to gather round my window and all I could do was try to wink and flirt back at them in the hopes of some earnings. It wasn't long for one guy to approach my window, in his strong accent he requested for a blow job and all his mates just cheered and applauded as I greeted him inside. By 8pm I had already had half a dozen clients, none of them were full intercourse just hand jobs and blow jobs. No matter what form of work I do on my clients, I always get them to wear a condom to protect myself, I have had the occasional guy who kicks off but I just show them the door if they are not happy to abide by my rules. It is not like I will go blurting to everyone what happens behind my closed curtains. My next client was not someone who I was expecting at all or to see anymore this evening. He approached towards my window with a straight look on his face, it was Dean. He had spruced himself up wearing a pair of smart denim blue jeans, an iron pressed white shirt and spiked up gelled hair. For a moment I just looked at him through the window, his face just remained straight and expressionless. Our gaze was then interrupted by one of the punters.

"Oi mate, are you going in or can I have my go with her."

"Sorry dude, I am booking her for the rest of the night." Dean reached into his pocket and pulled out a handful of Euros. The other punter soon made a brisk walk away. I opened the door to let Dean in, not understanding where he was going with this. As soon as he stepped inside, he quickly locked the door and shut all the curtains, the look on his face was still quite serious.

"Is everything ok?" I asked him worriedly.

"Sorry I just can't get over how sexy you look right now. I feel so jealous from these other blokes hanging around you."

"It doesn't mean anything to me, just work."

"I know, I know. Look I am not sure how much you want from me but please just spend the evening with me.

"Okay, let me ask Maria next door if she will cover for me." I finally gave up on wanting to try not doing anything with him. Maria was also from England like me, she was tall with long golden blonde hair and ocean blue eyes. Her family were originally from Italy so she had a European look about her, but she was born in the UK. Maria had been Sophie's best friend; they'd gone to school together then went travelling. Eventually Sophie and Maria became lovers and chose to live together in Amsterdam, however Sophie became addicted to heroin.

Chapter Five - Lucy

Sophie had a bit of a dark past, when she was fourteen years old, she was raped by Jack, the school's football captain. At the age of sixteen he should've known better about his actions. Sophie had developed quite fully from the age of thirteen, so Jack had taken an obsessed liking to her. He followed us sometimes when me and Sophie would walk home from school, so he quickly discovered where Sophie lived. She never told her parents about Jack following her home, but I think she believed he had a harmless crush on her. When she was fourteen her parents went away for a long weekend, I lived on the same street literally two doors down, so she knew if there were any issues, all she had to do was come see us or phone me. On the Saturday of that weekend, we had been to see a late movie with a mixed group of friends. The guys had offered to walk the ladies' home, right up to their front doors. James and Ben chose to walk with Sophie and myself, I had shared my first kiss with Ben that evening in the cinema. James and Sophie were going out, so it was ideal that those two walk back with us. As a teenager I was in ore on how perfect that night was, little did I know what was to come. I invited Ben in for a cola, so James walked with Sophie to her place, for an hour they sat on the doorstep just chatting, laughing, joking and sharing a couple of kisses. By then Ben had left mine and came for James so they could walk home together.

As poor Sophie let herself in, Jack had been hiding nearby and approached her, he carried a pocketknife and threatened to cut her if she didn't do what he said. He took her up to her bedroom and raped her, taking her virginity from her. Before he left the last thing, he said to her was 'now you are mine, bitch.'

Not long after it happened Sophie rang me in tears, begging me to come round and to bring my mum to. As soon as we stepped outside Jack was standing there shaking and at that very moment, I knew he was involved. I pushed passed him to get to Sophie's house, the front door was open ajar, and I could hear her crying upstairs. Mum ran ahead of me to Sophie's bedroom, as I followed close behind the image of her still haunts me today. My mum was amazing, I don't know how she managed to stay calm, but she just tried to comfort Sophie and keep her from screaming out loud. My mum requested I phone the police and make sure to mention the person responsible was outside. It didn't take the police long to arrive, fortunately Jack was still on our street, and he calmly let the police arrest him.

In police custody it took him hours until he decided to start talking, although he admitted what he had done, he tried to put some blame on Sophie by making out she was the one teasing him. Winking at him in the school corridors, blowing seductive kisses at him and secretly showing some cleavage to him. This was eventually taken to court, he wanted to see Sophie again as she was forced in a way to give evidence whilst testifying against him. The jury found him to be guilty, but he was also found to be not right of mind so was sentenced to have five years in a mental hospital.

Sophie got the help she needed to and eventually she was back to being her bubbly self again. Things didn't work out between her and James though, he felt guilty for leaving when he did that night, but it was no one's fault, no one could have predicted Jack being like that. When Sophie finished school at eighteen, both her and Maria went travelling together and they became a couple. Sophie was at her happiest prime falling for Maria, and I could not have been happier for them both.

However Sophie carried another dark secret, she had a drug problem. Maria knew she took the occasional one but didn't realise how extent it was.

The morning I found Sophie dead with a needle in her arm was just so heart breaking, she left a note stating Jack had found her. Turns out he'd come across her facebook profile and discovered she was living in Amsterdam. He had roamed the streets for a couple of days and seen she was working on the red-light district. He'd been watching her since and planned to have a moment with her once again. Whilst I was visiting Sophie I stayed at a nearby hotel, turns out Jack was staying in the same hotel as me. He'd been watching me as well, observing my every movement from leaving my hotel room to being with Sophie and Maria. He was making notes of when Sophie was working so he knew where to go and see her when she least expected it. So, when Sophie finished working that night, he had broke into her rented working room, she was cleaning down from her shift that night. As she turned round to see who it was, she recognised him. Sophie stated this in her final note, he had raped her again and this time he had left her a present, a huge dosage of heroin. Again, he had said to her 'you are mine, bitch.' Then he fled the scene, he'd left Amsterdam and went back to the

UK. This time round he'd gotten away with his crime, I believe he still he hadn't been caught and Sophie wasn't here to defend herself. That bastard took her from me.

Chapter Six - Lucy

Maria was happy to cover me that evening so I could go for dinner with Dean, I had covered for her the other week, so she wanted to repay me the favour. I was proud of Maria for coping with the loss of Sophie, she was the only girl I spoke with on the Red Light District. But with our busy working hours we both barely had the time to hang out, we always had each other's backs though if we needed cover. I shut my red curtains so I could make myself look more presentable. As it was quite a warm evening, I wore a pair of high waisted black shorts with a white crop top and to give my feet a rest, I put on a pair of flat sandals. Dean waited patiently outside for me until I was ready, in my handbag I packed a clean pair of lingerie and some condoms just in case things might happen again between us for one night only. I still kept telling myself that I I loved him so much and that I hadn't got over him.

As I stepped outside and locked the door to my rented working room, Dean came up to me and touched my right shoulder.

"You look incredible." He whispered into my right ear.

I just smiled back at him knowing that he liked what he saw. We headed to China town as I was in the mood for Chinese and I had tasted a couple of meals along there in some of the wonderful restaurants. Chinese was one of my all-time favourite meals so Dean knew where I would most likely go to eat. During our meal we caught up from the last moment we had together which was at the railway station in Kings Cross. He spoke about his family; I had asked how his parents were as he'd seen them a couple of times. But one question he did avoid to answer was how he was getting on in the army, he either chose to ignore me or changed the topic of our conversation. I found this to be quite odd but then as he was on annual leave, perhaps he didn't want to think of work.

After a lovely meal we went for a walk and headed to Suzi's Saloon bar. We drank plenty of Heineken in there as well as laughing and joking. Then in the heat of the moment Dean leaned forward towards me and kissed me softly on the lips.

"Sorry I shouldn't have done that."

However, inside I wanted it for longer, I'd missed his lips, his kisses over the past six months. It was so wonderful to feel him so close to me again and yet I was stunned. I couldn't let anyone see me like this out of work, what if Chris was still in the country. He'd been trying to get me to do things like this with him and I had always declined his offer. For Dean I was willing to break the rules for him, just to have a moment with him again. Maybe it was down to the few too many Heinekens why I felt this way, but I had to be back in Dean's arms again, even if it was just for that night.

After finishing our drinks in Suzie's Saloon bar, we took a stroll along by the canal under the starlight sky. It was just like a first date again, the moment of not knowing where things could lead on to from here.

"Do you fancy a drink in my room?"

His question took me away from my thoughts, was I ready to do this and let go of all the hurt and heartache from the last six months.

Chapter Seven - Lucy

Now here I was in his hotel room, a place I told myself I would never end up. He had changed rooms over from this morning when I had my shower as I did not recognise anything. This room was so spacious, open and very light. I guess I should've expected it to be like this at a Hilton Hotel, queen size bed with freshly quilted bedding, I had never come across a hotel room this big, not even the hotel room we had stayed in during our London weekend was anything like this. There was a lounge area with an Apple Mac set up and some files neatly stacked.

"I may be on annual leave, but I still can't keep away from my work." He spoke to me with a slightly nervous ton, he must've noticed my wondering eyes gazing around his hotel room.

The few Heinekens I'd been drinking back at Suzie's Saloon bar had gone to my head, but I felt strong urges for Dean. I didn't care what happened now as I just wanted to spend the night with him. This was breaking all my working rules but that wasn't going through my head at this very moment.

We had exchanged a couple of cheeky kisses in the bar, even though he apologised I still had to have his lips on mine again. Who cared what would happen tomorrow, I decided to live in the moment right now. Only Dean was the one who was nervous and couldn't look at me properly, he gently creaked his neck to see if that would try help him untense. I placed my hand on his left shoulder.

"Is everything ok?" I smoothly asked him.

For a moment, he just continued to look away from me, I wished I could've known what was going through his head right there and then. It was like he was in two minds whether or not to let this happen. I hoped he hadm't strung me along from the start and didn't want things to go any further.

I gently removed my hand from his left shoulder, I needed some water to clear my head a bit and try focus further more on this situation. Maybe I did not want this to happen deep down inside. The urges of longing for Dean's touch again were still lingering upon me. I really hoped he would make up his mind pretty quick if he wanted anything further to happen between us tonight. I spotted a glassed bottle of still water on the desk. My throat was parched so I headed over to the desk and took a sip of the cool clear liquid.

Dean then gave in and pulled me towards his firm torso, kissing me passionately like he never wanted to let me go. His hands moved to the base of my top and he gradually lifted it up, further and further until it finally went over my head. We moved over to the bed still trying to catch each other's lips whilst undressing each other. I perched on top of the quilt, with a seductive look in my lingerie, he had a cheeky grin now upon his face. We had got over the nerves and both knew we wanted this. I unclipped my bra and flung it to the floor, he crawled along the bed up to me and kissed my thighs moving up towards my bare breasts, caressing them causing a tingle in between my legs. He gently placed a couple of fingers down my knickers, feeling how excited he had gotten me, I hadn't felt like this with any of my clients. It was like my body had been waiting for Dean's touch to return to me, it had been longing, craving for him to be back with me, back inside of me.

"Wow." He said with an even bigger grin "It is so incredible to feel you again Lucy."

"I have missed you so much Dean." I could feel his erect penis pressing through his boxers over my pelvic area.

"Are you sure you want this?" I asked him for the last time.

He didn't answer, I could feel his excitement as he continued to kiss me and press his erection against me. I couldn't wait any longer and pulled down his boxers, kissing his manly hood and perching my lips on his tip.

"Oh my Lucy."

He gently pushed me away and reached for his jeans on the floor to pull out a condom, then he perched his lips back to mine as well as removing my panties. That night we made passionate love three times before then giving into exhaustion and drifting off to sleep…

Chapter Eight - Lucy

I naturally woke up the following morning after our wonderful night of passion, it had felt like sleeping with him for the very first time once again. His arms were round me and the sweat from all of our love making had clung our bodies together. Dean was still sleeping peacefully; I couldn't disturb him. The sun light was trying to break through the cracks in the curtains and the sound of faint voices were heard through the slightly open windows. I needed a caffeine boost so I decided to try and get up without disturbing Dean to head down to the hotel bar and see if they would bring us up some coffee to our room. I gently moved and unpeeled myself from Dean's firm embrace, he murmured but then rolled over and continued to gently snore away. Rolling out of the most snuggled duvet I have ever laid in, I reached for some form of clothing that was sprawled on the floor, a shirt that Dean had worn the night before until it was removed from our passionate moment undressing each other.

I tip toed to the ensuite bathroom, all sweaty and smelling of sex I needed a nice clean shower again.

As to not wake up Dean I crept back out into the room and gathered up all of my belongings and brought them into the bathroom. The warm water felt amazing cleansing upon my skin, the in house shampoo and shower gel gave my hair and body the clean that it needed but the memories after last night played over and over in my head. The love I had for Dean was reignited once again, could I really stay working on the red light district? Although I had just about paid off Sophie's debts, I still needed money to save up and come back to England. Maybe Dean could help me out with that? I just had to speak to him about my feelings and ask him the golden question of what happens between us now. I quickly showered myself down, used the hairdryer that was already connected in the ensuite bathroom. I just hoped the walls were soundproof. I had a brush buried at the bottom of my handbag with a bobble so I just yanked my hair up into a high pony tail.

Fully dressed and needing coffee, I slowly opened up the bathroom. Dean was still fast asleep. I then remembered to check in with Maria to see how she was after covering my shift for me. My phone battery was almost drained so I decided I would try access Dean's Apple Mac and login on facebook to send her a direct message from there. Of course it had to be password protected, so I tried a few of his old passwords and combinations from when we were together, after a few failed attempts I tried the last one I could think of, Lucy4ever<3<3.

Success I was logged in, his wallpaper was a photo of us both, but it was one I had not seen. It was a selfie that we took on the last day of our trip to London standing near the London eye, that was the last happy moment we had together before he broke up with me. But still I was touched that he had it on there as well as using my name for his password. Just as I was about to click the internet explorer icon, I noticed a file stored on his desktop named 'Kandi', turning back to the bed to check Dean was not waking up, curiosity got the better of me so I opened this peculiar file. Images of me flashed up on his screen of me walking alone through the streets of Amsterdam, then onto pictures of me standing in my working window. He knew all along about me working out here, how could he not tell me that. Pretending to be hurt seeing me working on the red light district. The words in my head at that moment just kept saying 'bastard.' But why though, why had he kept it from me? Dean hadn't been working in the army but for the Ministry Of Defence instead, now it all made sense as to why he never wanted to discuss with me about his work

I grabbed one of his files on the desk and started to browse through it, there were photos and documents on Chris. Who was Chris to him? There were photos of Chris entering and leaving my working room, one photo showed a little kiss that we once shared with each other, biggest mistake I did was let that happen. On one of the classified documents there was information about him running a few drug factories between Amsterdam and England, however there was something else I read that shocked me. Supposedly Chris was also funding the terrorist group Extinction Means War aka EMW. This was all too much for me, I could feel tears filling up in my eyes. It all made sense now why Dean was in Amsterdam, he had used me to try get closer to tracking down Chris. I was getting that worked up I could feel bile raising up to my throat, how could I have been so stupid to let Dean get too close back into my life again.

I left everything open on his desk, put on my shoes and ran out of the hotel room. I couldn't face him again.

Chapter Nine - Dean

I woke up after hearing the sound of a door slamming shut. My head felt fuzzy and confused full of juxtaposed moving images from the night before. An incredible night before I may add. I reached over to the other side of the bed for Lucy, but she was not there. I slowly lifted my head up to look for her, but she was nowhere in site. Damn I needed some water and a pain killer for this hangover. I grabbed for my boxer shorts I had worn the previous day and climbed out of bed. I noticed the bathroom door was closed and the extraction fan going, I knocked on the door.

"Lucy, are you in there?"

I tried the door handle, and it was unlocked, so I let myself into the ensuite bathroom. Wet footprints were scattered about and a couple of screwed up towels were slung in the corner, so she had been in here. I looked at myself in the mirror, blood shot eyes and ruffled up hair with a bruise on my lower neck, the fuck, it's a hickey. I should have known better than to allow this to happen at the age of twenty-six. I touched it though and just smiled, this was a mark to remind me of the most amazing and sexy woman I had sex with. I sort of hoped it will last a while, but I would have to wear a few alter neck tops at work until it vanishes. I splashed some water across my face to try wake up, damn where could Lucy be and how had I not heard her get up.

Walking out the bathroom I spotted my apple mac was open along with one of my files on the floor with its contents everywhere. Oh shit, I knew then it was her who had banged the door shut, Lucy had found out about who I worked for and the real reason I was here in Amsterdam. Fear struck me at that moment realising that she will think I had used her. That was not the case at all, I hadn't planned to bring Lucy back up here to just sleep with her. I still cared and loved her so much.

Breaking up with her just after Valentines Day, was one of the hardest decisions I had to make and one I still regret doing to this very day. I needed to find Lucy and fast, to explain everything to her. I searched for my mobile phone; it was still in my jeans pocket from the night before with a small amount of battery in it. I dialled her number, shit straight to voice mail. I placed my phone on charge whilst I rummaged through my hotel closet to put on something to wear. I could feel the heat on the sun reflecting from the curtains so I knew I would have to wear some shorts and a vest top.

Once dressed I grabbed my phone and room key then headed to the hotel lobby, as I stepped outside, I looked round to see if I could see her. My height was sort of an advantage as I could see over parts of the crowded street. I spotted her in the distance dodging and running round everyone, I yelled out her name, but she didn't stop or turn back round to look at me. I needed a shower myself from all the sweat of our passionate night, so I made the decision to head back to my room to sort myself out then I would track her down and make everything right. The one thing I would do was to get Lucy away from working on the red light district and help her get back onto her feet. It crushed me when I was given this assignment and finding out she was working out here. It angered and made me jealous to know she would have slept with many men, but after seeing her yesterday and hearing all about Sophie, I knew she had no choice. This Chris character though was definitely a threat for me, what if he wins over Lucy's heart then I would sure have lost her for good. That was something I was not going to let happen.

Chapter Ten - Lucy

The sun was blazing down on the city of Amsterdam, the crowds of people dressed up all colourful as they chose to and filled the streets. Everyone looked so happy and peaceful, I on the other hand needed to get as far away as possible. I asked a nearby tourist for the time, it was almost noon. 'Shit' I had to be ready for work in an hour, it was going to be a struggle getting through these crowds of people. The canal was full of different boats decorated up ready for the pride parade that would be starting up at one.

I just ran through the crowds of people and did not look back, I even thought I heard my name faintly being shouted. Perhaps Dean had woke up finally and discovered I found out the truth of everything. The tears began to fall down my cheeks whilst trying to dodge the people partying out on the streets. I needed a drink of water again; the sun was too high up and hardly any shade but I just carried on running. As soon as I got past the canal, I didn't think to check on any on coming vehicles and I ran straight into a cyclist. Before he had chance to yell at me, I chucked him twenty euros and then carried on running. My legs were scuffed and bleeding, but I didn't have time to stop and clear them up, I needed to get back to my working room.

From a distance spotting my room something didn't look right about it, as I got closer I realised it'd been broken into. This day couldn't get any worse now, I slowed my pace to walking and just headed through the smashed in door of my working room. It was a mess; my makeup was scattered everywhere, and my laptop had gone as I would have expected it to. My fancy outfits and lingerie sets had been pulled out of my drawers and slung about. Luckily, I hadn't kept any of my money hidden away, I had put it all in my purse and kept it all on me when I was out the night before. Kneeling down, placing my hand on to one of my under garments I just let the tears fall and fall, my heart was hurting again from Dean. I wish I could just turn back time, not to have let Chris leave my room yesterday morning as I would not have gone out for our walk round the canal which then led onto other things. I could not grasp the idea on Dean working for the MOD and Chris funding terrorism then heading back to my room and it being completely turned over.

Footsteps approached behind and the snap of shattered glass from each step entering my room. I didn't want to face whoever it was, sick of men right now especially Dean. I felt a soft gentle hand stroking the top of my head, it was not a touch I was familiar with. Whoever it was, crouched by the side of me and handed over some tissues. I gave in and looked to see who it was, of all people it was Maria, the one person I was happy to see.

"Oh Lucy I am so sorry." She spoke to me smoothly; she wrapped her arms round me trying to comfort me in the best way she possibly could. I just let the tears continue to fall, I really missed Sophie so much and it was moments like this where I needed my family especially my mum.

"Are you ready to go?" Maria asked me.

I nodded and searched for my little suitcase to try gather up what I could. I was not able to stay here or work today so I would try and find a little hotel room tonight to gather my thoughts. On rummaging through my belongings, I found a framed picture of Sophie that was in the bottom drawer of my lingerie sets. I glanced at it for a moment, remembering everything from the small amount of time we had together in this life. Maria was also looking at the photo with me and I could see the tears welling up in her eyes, it was clear her heart still belonged to Sophie. We hugged and cried into each other's arms.

"Do you think Jack will ever be found?" I asked her.

"I really do hope so. I just want him to have justice for what he has done." Although she answered me softly, I could feel her tense up talking about Jack.

We still cuddled for another moment; it was nice to have a friend who cared about me in the city. I don't have anything else to do with the other ladies on the red light district.

"Right let's get you packed and find somewhere to lay low for the rest of the day."

I packed the photo of Sophie into my suitcase along with whatever clothing I could find that hadn't been ripped up. Once I was all sorted, we left my working room and headed to the shops. My stomach was rumbling away, I needed to get some food and drink quite soon before I ended up passing out. The first place I spotted for food was the New York Pizza place, I remembered Sophie taking me here on the day I landed in Amsterdam to grab a quick bite to eat. The smell of cooked dough lingered through the shop which caused my tummy to rumble again. There was a small round table and two chairs empty in the corner, so I placed my suitcase on one of the chairs and joined the back of the queue. There were only three other people in front of me, so I didn't have to wait too long, this area of Amsterdam had quietened down compared to normal as everyone had made their way to the canal as the parade was now well on its way. For ten euros you could grab two pizza slices and a drink, I was gagging for a cold drink so I chose a can of cola to go with my two slices of pepperoni pizza. Maria did the same and headed to the table in the corner.

As we were sat down and tucking into our food, I told her all about Dean and what I had discovered that morning, although she'd never met him apart from a brief glimpse of him from last night, she still believed he truly loved me. I wanted this to be true but inside something kept telling me to have my whit's about him. The pizza slices however did help to comfort my breaking heart, what was it about pizza that just knew how to perk you up when you are feeling down.

"Oh, I forgot to give you this." Maria reached into her jacket pocket and pulled out a power pack so I could charge up my phone.

"You are an angel."

I reached for my handbag and pulled out my mobile phone, it had run out of battery as I hadn't been in my room last night. I connected it up to the power pack and just let my phone gain some charge.

"Last night after I finished, I saw a couple of guys in black suits patrolling round. They seemed to hover nearby, mainly around our rooms too."

"Do you think it was them who might've broke into my room?"

"Quite possibly."

"Do you think you would recognise them again?"

"Yes, as one of them had a tribal tattoo on the right side of his face."

That was a good start to know Maria would at least recognise one of them again if she saw them in the street. They may have just been at the wrong place at the wrong time but whoever these guys were, it was obvious they were looking for something or someone.

Chapter Eleven - Maria

Seeing Lucy so crushed hit me pretty hard, she is the closest connection I have to Sophie. Poor Lucy has been through so much trauma over the past six months and I had always held it to be my responsibility to look out for her. I never realised how much debt Sophie had built since we moved to Amsterdam and dearest Lucy felt the need to work hard and pay it off. Both of her parents and Sophie's parents still to this day do not know about her drug problem, I offered to Lucy that I would pay it off, but she was adamant that she was to do it as she knew I had my own cost of living to pay for. Now and again, I did treat her to new clothes and some small luxuries as a way of saying thank you but we both very rarely had the time to go out together. This was a once in a blue moon opportunity that we hung out together away from our working lives, it was nice to be able to do this. Sitting inside New York Pizza in the corner away from familiar faces who are used to seeing us in our working windows felt good for a change. After Lucy telling me all about Dean working for the MOD, I was sort of not surprised, I knew about him from the start and I had that feeling he must be working as something top secret to end their relationship after a perfect weekend away. Still, he was a jerk for choosing to make these decisions and also keeping secrets from her too. At least Lucy's secret that she kept from him was to help out Sophie and me, she had good intentions for doing what she did.

I was even more shocked to discover Chris' background as well, he had spent the odd hour or so with me if Lucy was not available. He very rarely slept with me, mainly he just paid for my time to sit and chat whilst he waited for Lucy to be free. I know he some connection for her, as mostly his conversations were about Lucy and how he hopes to whisk her away, but she never seemed interested in him. To her, he was just a regular client that was helping to fund her getting back to England. I was also saving up to go back to England with Lucy too, although I do love Amsterdam it holds too many painful memories. The last time we were in England was for Sophie's funeral, however we could only stay there for one night as we had to be on the first plane back the following morning to ensure we were there to start work. Lucy's mum had booked for us, a nearby Premier Inn as our last minute flight prices cost too much. It was nice of her mum to pay for us to stay, she even offered to cover the cost for us to stay a week, but we just couldn't. I knew Lucy's mum had some debts of her own to pay off as Lucy's dad had a motorbike accident a few years ago. Although it wasn't his fault, the legal case is still ongoing at this moment in time.

I couldn't get the guy with the tattoo face from off my mind, I noticed him gazing to me when I was out working last night. Both him and his colleague had walked past about five times before I finished my shift at one this morning. The last time I saw him was when I locked up my room, checked Lucy's was locked up and headed straight for my one-bedroom apartment nearby. I felt drawn to him every time our eyes made contact, there was some connection I had to me. Before I had finished for the night Chris had approached my window, he had come to see Lucy as he was heading home today, he paid for my time to sit in my room to chat with me for the last half an hour. He did seem a bit odd like questioning about Lucy's whereabouts and what she was up to. I simply just had to say she was having a rare night off as she needed one and was out with a friend. I had to try and find the right moment to tell Lucy about this. Chris was a good-looking guy and if her heart didn't still belong to

Dean, I reckon she would have eventually got with him.

Chapter Twelve – Lucy

It was so nice to be with Maria, I felt relieved getting things off my chest. As soon as we had finished our food, we decided to head to the shops for a little retail therapy before we then marched on to find an available hotel room. Maria didn't want to go back to her apartment either, she wanted to make sure I was going to be fine so we would do some shopping and then head to her place to grab an overnight bag. On passing by Waterstones, I spotted Dean in the distance searching for someone and with his phone out as though he was tracking something. I grabbed hold of Maria's arm.

"Shit there's Dean, I can't face him right now."

"Let's hide in here. Quick."

She pulled me into Waterstones and headed towards the back of the store where the young adult section was. There we picked up a book each and pretended like we were browsing, at the corner of our eyes we gazed towards the door and the open windows and waited for Dean to pass by.

"Phew that was a close call." I said letting out a big sigh of relief.

"I am presuming he is looking for you or he is searching for Chris."

"Perhaps maybe both of us."

We waited a few more moments to make sure Dean didn't come back, once we felt like the coast was clear, we purchased a book each and left the shop. Gazing to the left and then the right, we kept our heads down and carried on walking along the high street. I just wished this area had more of a busier crowd so we could be more hidden away, I couldn't deal with seeing either Dean or Chris. For all I cared at this moment, men can just fuck off and I was going to remain being single. The heart break of the past six months began to build a weight upon me and the tears of all the pain filled my eyes. Maria squeezed my hand as she let me cry a few tears in the middle of the street, she then pulled me in for a cuddle to try comfort me. I heard her sniffling to, I believed she was thinking about Sophie again, we were both so heartbroken. The sound of a wolf whistle interrupted our thoughts as a male tourist ran up to us and dived right in between us. He stank of beer and weed.

"Hey you beautiful ladies." He slurred in his half drunken up British accent.

"Watch it." Maria snapped back at him.

We divided ourselves away from the tourist, as we moved, he stumbled to the ground and laughed out loud, his mates then staggered round and helped their friend back to his feet. Maria linked arms with me as we walked away from this group of guys, it was already a bad day for men, and I couldn't be doing with anymore idiots at the moment.

"Hey girls, where're you going?" We carried on walking away from the group of hooligans trying to attract our attention, they continued to yell at us but we both kept our backs turned and not give them the satisfaction. As we headed to the end of the street, I did have a quick glance behind me and spotted two policeman had approached the group of tourists, thank goodness as that would be the end of all that commotion.

"Tourists." I just blurted out to Maria.

"Bunch of knob heads." She snorted back to me.

"Of course, we just can't help being so gorgeous."

We both needed a giggle after that very awkward moment, normally when we get attention like that, we are standing in our windows and doorways so we can just normally shut the door or pull the curtain across, and that would be the end of it. But being in the street, getting attention like that was often nerve wracking as we didn't have so much as a defence shield. In the distance Maria spotted Dean walking on the opposite side of the street, thank goodness for her being so tall, I was always at a disadvantage only being 5ft 5in in height. I managed to then see Dean as he got nearer within my eyeline, seeing him from a distance I still noticed how good looking he was but after what I found out this morning, I didn't want anything to do with him.

"We need to make a move before he sees us."

There was a nearby passageway where we headed towards, before Dean spotted us, barely any sunlight reached through the cracks into this passageway, the smell of marijuana was replaced with the linger of blocked drains. Although it stank too much for my nostrils to take in, I was relived to be out of Dean's eyesight. We stopped to catch our breath quickly but not to loiter to much from how bad the drains were. An opening was straight to the other side and that was the direction we walked to. As soon as we got to the opening, we were ambushed and as everything happened so quickly, things turned black.

Chapter Thirteen - Lucy

Five days later……

I turned the key in the lock and opened the door whilst recapping through my mind the past week on what I'd gone through. To my horror, I saw Chris standing there, waiting for only me. The last thing I remembered was being back in the cultured city of Amsterdam hiding with Maria from Dean, my ex-boyfriend. I'd just spent a night of passion with him back in his hotel room when, I discovered the main reason why he was back in Amsterdam. I'd been so stupid to believe Dean wanted me back which just bought on further pain to my never-ending broken heart. Now I was on some sort of secret cruise ship, owned by Chris. He was one of my regular clients to visit me in my working room along the red light district, he would always pay me five hundred euros per night to book my services so no one else could have me. Chris had often asked me to his hotel room, but I'd always refused as it was my number one rule, to never sleep with the clientele during outside of working hours. It would no doubt lead to complications especially with Chris as I knew he wanted me, but I had no feelings towards him especially now I'd seen Dean again.

Now he was behind this locked door, to his secret bed chamber where no one else was allowed to enter unless you were gifted a key. In this case I'd been gifted one, it was left for me inside the bed chamber where I had been placed in on the day we were taken hostage. Maria was locked in the room next door, we only saw each other when our services were called to entertain the men on board the cruise ship, normally during after their evening meals but we were not allowed to be touched, as we both were there just for show. We'd been looked after with clothes, being fed by the house keeping staff and waiting staff but our rooms were always guarded by two bouncers.

The look on Chris' face was not his usual friendly and polite smile, his eyes were filled with rage and his posture was positioned animal, like as though he wanted to pounce on me anytime. I took a deep breath and shut the door gently behind, tonight's outfit request was to wear a golden glittery bra and thong set that he had arranged one of the housekeeping staff to place onto my king size bed.

"Lock the door please." He spoke to me with a stern tone.

I did as I was commanded and remained quiet, he ushered for me to move closer towards him. As I walked close enough, he gently grabbed my right hand and pressed his lips to it. I couldn't look him straight in the eye, from his body language he was not happy with me, and I suspected that it had been Chris all along taking us hostage, before we hid in that secluded alley, I'd ran up to my working room to see it had been broken into and trashed. Maria had been working in the room next door to mine but luckily, she had finished her shift before this happened. But Maria had seen their faces who did it lurking around, she was their key witness when the police would arrive to investigate what had happened.

Chris' eyes moved up and down.

"You do look beautiful as always my dear Lucy." He said huskily to me.

I still couldn't bring myself to look into his eyes, normally his eyes were full of kindness but tonight they were a look of anger. He must've found out I had spent the night with Dean in his hotel room. Chris must have known who Dean was, an agent for the Ministry of Defence out to hunt him and bring him in. Dean had obviously used me to try get closer to tracking down Chris, but it had backed fired as I found a file containing details and photos of myself as well as Chris. I'd discovered that Chris' henchmen were searching through my working room, Maria took hold of my arm to usher me to be off the red light district asap as it wasn't safe for us to be out in the open. We must've been followed by the same henchmen, when both Maria and I were safe walking up a small alleyway that was derelict, the henchman blocked our route out and must've took us both hostage. Whilst I was in and out of consciousness, we were warned to act naturally whilst entering a limo parked nearby with blacked out windows, sitting for two hours not knowing where we were going until the car stopped outside the cruise ship with no logos on it anywhere. We were at Rotterdam ports, and this was how I'd ended up here in Chris' bed chamber.

Chapter Fourteen - Maria

I can't remember how long ago it was when Lucy and I were kidnapped from Amsterdam. Each day that passes by for me is just a blur, it's as though the days merge into one. Every night I cry still for the passing of Sophie, she is always on my mind. I fell in love with Sophie for who she was as a person. Before we developed our relationship, I'd never been with a girl before. I chose to be pansexual when my feelings towards Sophie grew and grew. The first time we kissed was during a calm evening stroll along Gentleman's Canal in Amsterdam, the sky was a clear starry night sky. The moment couldn't have been more perfect for us. The city of Amsterdam was the ideal place for us to settle and live here for a while. The first moment we made love was incredible, Sophie had an experimental encounter when she was in her teens, and I didn't have any experience at all. But she knew exactly how to pleasure me. She proposed to me straight away on our first Christmas morning together as a couple and I said yes in a heartbeat. We didn't have a lot of money but the ring she bestowed me was from Pandora, it was silver and shaped like a bow. The ring was perfect enough for me. I would give anything just to have her for another day, kiss her one more time and feel her touch once again. I truly miss Sophie so much; she was my first real love and she will always have a place in my heart.

I think I must've been crying louder than I realised as the next thing I heard was a knock at my door and all my thoughts of Sophie temporarily vanished.

"Maria, are you ok in there?"

As I heard the male voice call those words out to me, I was transferred back into the room on this private cruise ship, Chris' private cruise ship, he must have a lot of money. It wasn't Chris' voice at the door. Climbing off the bed that was layered in silk bedding, I headed for the door and tried the handle. As usual it was locked.

"Who is it?" I called back through my tears.

The sound of a bunch of keys was heard rummaging until the lock was released. I tried the door handle again and this time it opened. On the other side of the door was one of the guards who took Lucy and me from that alleyway in

Amsterdam, when we were hiding from Dean. It was the man with the tribal tattoo down his face.

"Is everything ok?" he asked me.

"Yes I'm fine." Whilst wiping the tears away.

"Can I come in?"

I moved away from the door and sat down on the chair by the dressing table, reaching for the nearest brush and thread it through my long blonde wavy hair. I tried to hide my tear-stained face from the guard, not wanting him to know much of my business. I felt his warm hand touch my bare shoulder as though he was trying to comfort me. Something strange aroused through me from his warm touch, a similar sensation from the first time I held hands with Sophie. It was as though I was drawn to him. He placed a finger under my chin and gently moved my face up to look into his hazel eyes, I couldn't look away from his kind gaze.

"I'm sorry if this is too far." He nervously spoke to me, confused by his words of what he meant. The next moment he perched his lips onto mine, unexpectedly I welcomed his kiss for a moment then I thought of Sophie once again. I gently pushed him away.

"I can't do this."

He looked slightly hurt and embarrassed which made me feel even worse.

"I'm just not ready for this, I lost the love of my life just over six months ago and I'm still struggling to move on from it."

"Oh shit, I'm so sorry Maria, forgive me for intruding." He moved away and headed for the door, without thinking I chased after him to stop him.

"Please don't go, I would appreciate some company until I have to start work later on."

He stopped in his tracks and turned round to look at me, his facial features formed a friendly smile, I noticed the cheeky dimple on his right cheek which made him very cute. There was just something about him that I was drawn to.

"I'm Tye by the way."

Holding out his right hand, I reciprocated with mine and we shook hands.

"Nice to meet you, Tye." Smiling back at him.

"Did you want to talk about why you were crying?" He asked me concerned.

It was wonderful to know someone actually wanted to chat with me, about my feelings instead of just paying to have my time on sexual favours. After all I am still a person and not just a sex worker. We both perched on the end of the bed, he placed his hand on top of mine as I went through what happened with Sophie and how she was raped at fourteen, to us falling in love, Lucy coming to visit and how Sophie ended her life. As I got to this part of my story I choked back tears, not coping very well on losing Sophie once again. Tye held me in his broad arms whilst I let the tears fall and fall.

Chapter Fifteen - Dean

It's been nearly a week now since I lost Lucy once again, I'd been so foolish to have left my work file out on display. I do wish she hadn't snooped around but I guess I broke her heart once before so any woman would've done the same. I still love her so much, but I let my work get in the way. I saw her get kidnapped by Chris' henchmen and I was determined to get her back. I will get her away from this working life and set up home back in England right where she belongs. I'm not going to lose her again, if it comes to it fuck this ministry of defence job, my heart has been broken more than enough now. Lucy is the love of my life and who I choose over everything. Whilst deep in my thoughts, my phone beeps. Someone who I work with had planted a tracking device on Chris' secret cruise ship, as I touch the app on my phone, it locates a dot right in the middle of the Atlantic Ocean. I make a few phone calls to my other colleagues to try plan our next course of action, I need to take down Chris and rescue my girl. The thought of him having his way with her out there and for all these months angers me, I am to blame for her crossing paths with this terrorist leader and getting roped into working on the red light district. I should've been there for her when she lost Sophie but instead, I chose to remain tracking down Chris, my ego got the better of me when instead I should've followed my heart. Clenching my fists to the point where my nails dug into my skin drawing out blood, I've never been so angry. Heading out of the balcony from my hotel window, I look up at the starry night sky, something about stars just seem to bring me hope and tranquil. No wonder Van Gogh painted about a starry night sky, reaching into my jean pocket, I pull out a cigarette and spark up whilst deep in my thoughts on how to try and rescue the love of my life. I do hope she is keeping strong and wonder if I cross her thoughts at all, knowing that I will be coming for her as soon as I can. Lucy if you can hear my thoughts, please know I do still truly love you.

Chapter Sixteen - Lucy

After last night with Chris, I've truly come to the point now where I despise that man. He has kidnapped me and now wants me as his own possession, for no one else to have. Although I hate Dean for using me, I do still truly love him so much and that I hope he will come for me. But as he is so selfish I doubt he will do; his work has always been more important to him than having me in his life. I loved our night of passion we last spent together, but I know it meant nothing to him, he just wanted to get closer to me on trying to track down Chris. But yet, I still long for him. I've cried so much in this room since acknowledging that I've been taken hostage and used for entertainment on Chris' private cruise ship. There is only so much crying and moping about that I can do now; I will just have to accept for the time being that this is my life on board somewhere in the middle of the Atlantic Ocean.

Deep in my thoughts, a faint knock on my door just about interrupted me, it was a gentle tap, instantly I guessed it will be Maria seeing if I'm ready to head to the casino, to prance around all of Chris' private guests on board his cruise ship. I open the door a jar just to make sure it was her, instantly I noticed her long golden flowing hair. Happy to know it was her I opened my room door fully, close behind her was one of Chris' henchmen. Maria must've seen the worried look flash upon my face.

"It's ok, Tye is a friend, he's been looking after me."

A huge sign of relief knowing he wasn't sent by Chris to come and collect me to then take him back to his bed chamber yet again.

"Before you both head down I need to chat to you, Kandi, is it ok if we just go into your room?"

I stepped back away from the door to let them both inside. Tye swiftly shut the door as he was last to enter, then checked round my bed chamber to see if there were any bugs or wires. Once he was happy, he gestured for Maria and myself to sit down.

"I'm working undercover for the UK ministry of defence."

"Don't tell me, you were sent by my ex, Dean."

"Not exactly, we were both assigned this mission together. I shouldn't be sharing this with you but for your safety I feel I must. Chris has been secretly funding a terrorist organisation known as Extinction Means War. This evening, he will be hosting an event in their honour. I plan to take this terrorist group down tonight but I'm going to need you both to work with me. At least for your own safety. I've finally managed to alert Dean our exact coordinates, as well as my colleagues back in England so help will be coming."

This all sounded to surreal for me to take in, I hadn't thought much more about the case file I'd glanced through back in Dean's hotel room, but now it all became clear. I wasn't going to be Chris' play thing anymore, regardless on his wealthy income he spent on me trying to help, knowing he was an evil man bought up bile to my throat. I couldn't hold it in and sprinted across to the ensuite bathroom to let it all out.

"Lucy." I heard Maria calling my name, "Are you ok in their chicka?"

After I'd stopped being sick, I plonked myself down on the floor with the thoughts of an evil man touching my body. Maria came into the bathroom with a bottle of ice-cold water and perched down beside me. She held me, this was comforting that she understood my thoughts.

"I miss Sophie, I miss Dean and I hate Chris."

These were the words I murmured out as I took a sip from the cool liquid, the condensation clenched my clammy fingertips and soothing the burning sensation from my throat. I took a second sip only this time it aggravated my throat, coughing and spluttering with the need of wanting to be sick again. Maria patted my back to try calm me down, another sip of water and I'd finally come to my senses. This was all too much for me, but I knew what must be done. Another tap at the bathroom door, this time it was Tye.

"Are you both ok in there?"

Maria looked to me, I nodded gently to let her know I was fine and to open the door.

"Yes, we're fine." Said Maria gracefully, it was nice she had a connection with someone else, though I feared her heart may get broken again. She may not physical be related to me, but I classed her as family. A sister I never had. Tye held out his hand to help me to my feet, I liked that he had manners for a lady.

"Cheers, sorry I had a wobble."

"It's cool, just I need to know if you're going to be fine for this evening."

"Oh I will be, first I'm going to take down Chris then I need to clear the air with Dean."

We sat back inside my bed chamber and listened to instructions from Tye to what his plan was.

Chapter 17 – Lucy

Hair and make-up - check

Golden sequin leotard with thong base - check

Fake tan topped up - check

Golden Stilettos - check

I was all set, ready to start my shift in this evening's grand casino hall where Chris will be hosting his big event. As usual it was a request for myself and Maria to wear the most revealing of outfits ever, an advance cash payment was placed outside our chamber doors before heading out into the grand hall. I had a small briefcase hidden under my bed where I locked inside all of my wages, since being on board this cruise ship. If I ever get back to England, I would ensure I'd pay this into my bank account. Luckily in Amsterdam I was able to make regular cash pay ins to my bank account from being a working girl.

I stepped outside my bed chamber, to be greeted by Maria waiting out in the landing for me, close by was Tye. I glanced at him; he was oblivious to me as he was eyeing up Maria. Least he only had eyes for her out of the two of us, brownie points for him on this occasion. Tye escorted us both down to the main entrance doors to the grand casino hall.

"Are you both ready?" We nodded, this was it, I just had to keep Chris and his guests entertained until Dean and the Ministry of Defence showed up to hijack this event. Walking through the double doors, my head held up high, a pose as an influx of Chris' guests surrounded us to take photos. Tye and a couple of other bodyguards were standing close by as to not allow anyone to go near us, no one was allowed to pose with us under the strict instructions of Chris. However, one of the punters, a cocky Caucasian male about 6 ft did sneak past Tye and approached close to me.

"Hey there pretty lady, fancy a quickie with me."

His remarks towards me were disgusting, I kept my cool and just smiled politely towards him. Keeping my cheeks firm, not making it obvious that I was really uncomfortable.

"No thank you, please go back to where you were sitting."

The punter moved very close to me, to the point I can smell his alcohol fuelled breath upon me. I knew it wouldn't be long until Chris intervened and that will be this punter's biggest mistake.

"Please just go back to your seat."

"How much for the full works pretty lady?"

The sound of a gunshot was heard followed by a loud screech as though someone was in pain, the punter collapsed to the ground gripping hold of his leg. Blood from his wound had splattered across my bare legs, luckily no blood landed on my outfit, just a tiny speck gushed onto my lower lip. Still, it made me nauseous. A firm arm clung round me, the smell of gunpowder filled the air around me, as I gazed towards the person who tugged his arm round me and a rifle, recently fired came to view.

"You mother fucker." The punter yelled out.

"Touch Kandi again, it will be your life next time. Consider that as a warning shot." Chris had shot him; it would appear I am one of his prized possessions that no one else can lay their hands on. Chris wiped away the speck of blood on my lower lip with a delicate handkerchief.

"Are you alright Kandi?" Chris asked me with a concerned look upon his face.

"Yes I'm fine." I replied quietly.

The screeching noise from the punter still rung through my ears, although he was in the wrong, I still empathised towards him. The poor bloke had drunk too much already and most likely wasn't fully aware of his actions. A simple shove would've sufficed just to get this man away from me.

"Get him out of my site." Chris ordered towards Tye.

Tye and another one of the bodyguards helped to lift the punter away, a thin blood trail followed behind them from his wound. Chris clicked his fingers for one of the waiting staff to come and mop up the red residue from off the floor. Another waiter followed behind with dry towels to try wipe away the wetness from the mop. Chris signalled towards the bar staff to usher them out with more drinks to everyone, due to the inconvenience from the incident. Within moments, various staff were carrying out trays of pornstar martini cocktails complimented with a shot of champagne, all were on the house but then I guess Chris had enough money. By the thought of money, Chris slipped something through my leotard at the top of my pelvic area.

"A little something extra for you too my love."

I gave him a small smile but inside I just wanted to vomit, I wasn't his love. Whatever feelings I may had felt towards Chris had long gone now.

"May I go freshen up?" I asked him quietly.

"Of course, you can but please don't be too long, I need you for my entertainment. Tye please escort Kandi to her room."

Tye nodded and ushered me away. His clothing covered in blood stains from carrying the punter away. As he exited the door, Tye had grabbed hold of Maria to come along with us. Chris most likely wouldn't have kept as much of a close eye on Maria because his usual focus was always where I was and what I was up to. We entered my bed chamber; Tye locked the door behind him.

"Right listen to me, I have received a message from Dean, he's about to board this cruise vessel. He will await my signal first before taking any action, I have no idea how he will make his entrance but be on full alert. Things are about to get messy especially that a couple of agents are under water now with the Navy."

My heart skipped a beat, knowing I was about to see Dean anytime this evening made me nervous. But no matter what, I was looking forward to seeing him.

"I best make myself look decent then." I smiled cheekily at both Maria and Tye. "Especially that I'm about to see the man I love once again."

Without my knowledge, Tye had an open line on his radio, Dean heard what I said.

Chapter 18 - Dean

Just enough to hear Lucy say she loves me was the main focus on this mission being worthwhile, if it wasn't for her, I probably would've had another agent carry on this mission for me. I was stupid to have let her go in the first place; I had my chance back in Amsterdam to make things right, but I blew it. Now this was my last opportunity to fix things and prove to her once and for all that I do truly love her. I've been a dickhead through and through. As I heard her say *Especially that I'm about to see the man I love once again* A smile rose upon my face along with a tear to my right eye. After how I've treated her, she still loves me and I still love her.

Tye had given the go ahead for me to board the cruise vessel, I just hope I wasn't too late for Lucy to have come to any harm. Sneaking through the dark starboard side, I was armed and ready. A couple of guardsmen were patrolling nearby towards the direction I was heading. I stealthily took them out one by one, enough to knock them out. I try to avoid killing anyone, especially since I was in the army, I try not to reflect much on those past times during my military career path. I only think back on the times I was with Lucy, its always about her.

On high alert now as I draw close to my entrance, I was going to gatecrash this party, the nerves itched at me not knowing what quite to expect as I make my move. All the other agents were in place, a handful disguised as guards inside the casino hall, a few outside waiting to break in. Standing above the casino hall, I glanced through the ceiling window, with its dome shape appearance but trying not to make a sound. Looking down at everyone, the guests were all drinking, smoking and taking whatever to get a thrill. I spotted her, all glammed up wearing a gold sequinned leotard, it did look quite revealing too revealing for her to be wearing in a room full of men. Stood right next to her was Chris, keeping a close eye on her whilst she is just standing there, hand on hip putting on a brave face.

"Dean, wait for my signal." I heard Tye's voice through my earpiece.

I did as I was instructed, holding my ground but the urge to break in was becoming too intense. Still gluing my eyes on Lucy and Chris nearby, moving right at her, stroking his fingers through her hair with his left hand then his right hand touching the top of her right thigh. The jealous rage inside of me was getting stronger and stronger now, no one touches my girl.

"Tye, I'm going in."

"No, not y…"

Before he could finish his objection, I smashed through the glass dome, abseiling into the casino hall, shards of glass rained everywhere but I didn't care now, I was beyond caring what anyone thinks. I probably will be disciplined for my actions for not waiting, but I wanted this prick away from her. As I fly in mission impossible style, a few of the guardsmen opened fire on me, the undercover agents had my back and opened fire back on them. I did a few warning shots as well to try get them to back off. I landed on the ground with both feet, I unclipped my harness and fixed my eyes onto Chris.

"Well well well, it seems like the ex-boyfriend has decided to gatecrash." Chris sniggered at me.

Lucy looked in shock upon my entrance, I gave her a cheeky wink. I noticed a brief smirk appear on her face.

"I'm here to take you down Chris, you are wanted for crimes to plot terrorism."

At a blink of an eye, Chris held out his gun pointing towards me.

"Go ahead shoot me, it's not going to stop me. Your vessel is surrounded, I suggest you surrender."

He grabs hold of Lucy to have her hostage. She cries out for help.

"Ask your agents to lower their weapons or I blast your sweethearts brains out."

I froze for a moment trying to grasp in what to do next. Adrenaline kicking in now, heart racing but I kept my cool.

"Let her go, she has nothing to do with any of this."

"She does though, its always you she pines for. No matter how much I've tried to take care of her, its always you she thinks about. You don't deserve her."

"No, I don't deserve her, I agree with you. I've never treated Lucy how she deserves to be treated. I was never there for her during the loss of Sophie when I should've been."

I noticed Lucy flinch when I mentioned about her late cousin, even Maria let out a loud sob when I mentioned her name. Tye held Maria softly as she collapsed to the floor. The wounds of Sophie's death still hadn't been healed, a tragic story of a victim who never had justice for what she went through, my next mission would be to get the justice of this case, I know this would mean the world to Lucy. I noticed the tears fall down her soft rosy cheeks, this was enough to cut me deep.

"Tye, shoot him." Chris yelled.

Tye took out his gun, for a moment he did aim it at me, Chris still holding Lucy hostage. I just wanted to comfort her and allow her to cry on my shoulder. The sound of a gunshot was heard, the bullet flew past my left ear, just brushing past my hair through a guardsman who snuck up behind me holding a knife. The bullet landed straight through his head, a splatter of blood shot to the floor with reminisce of skull fragments and flesh.

"You traitor." Chris barked at Tye "You no good double crosser."

"Just shows I'm very good at my job, sir." Tye smirked back at Chris.

I still had my eyes locked on Lucy; I don't know what came over her but I saw the range grow upon her face. I hadn't expected what she planned to do but her mouth widened, and her teeth clung onto Chris's arm. She bit him so hard that she drew blood, causing Chris to release his grasp and drop his gun. Blood dripping from her lips, she knelt down and picked up his gun aiming it right at Chris.

"You psycho bitch." Chris screeched at her whilst in pain from his fresh wound.

She just glared at him, no reaction to his insult at her. Fixed in stance still aiming to shoot him, cocking the gun.

"If you're going to shoot me, I suggest you do it now and get it over and done with."

I walked over to her side.

"Lucy, you don't need to shoot him. He's lost, we can now arrest him."

She still didn't move, specks of blood still dripped from her mouth from the wound she caused on Chris. I didn't know what she was thinking.

"Don't call me a psycho bitch."

After a moment, I touched he left arm, she flinched but then welcomed my touch and relaxed her arm. I took hold of the gun as two agents approached Chris and handcuffed him. Lucy collapsed but I held her tightly and kissed her forehead.

"It's over now." I whispered into her ear.

"Please just take me home." Lucy pleaded with me.

We gazed into each other's eyes, I moved in to kiss her lips, her lips were happy to receive mine as our kiss transpired passionately. I'd missed her deeply.

Chapter 19 - Lucy

The helicopter ride home was nice, Dean held onto me all the way back to England. Although there were no words, I embraced the moment to be in his arms once again. I didn't want it to end. Landing back on a secluded air base, we were escorted to a highly guarded bunker to clean up. I was shown into a room where some clean clothes had been placed onto the bed, not appealing ones but enough to be fully covered. The shower room was just straight down the hallway. That was the first place I headed to, right next to the clothes on the bed was a toiletry pack and some towels. I grabbed them all and headed to the showers. I couldn't wait to get out of this skimpy outfit, I had a quick glance at the mirror over a sink basin to see how much of a mess I looked. Chris' blood had dried upon my lips, mascara smudged over my eyes and my hair was tangled. I looked a mess. Stripping off naked I slung the leotard into a nearby bin and walked into the communal shower room. The hot water was bliss as it flowed over my body, I thought I heard the sound of a lock being triggered but I was deep in my thoughts as I wasn't prepared to be questioned. Opening my eyes I saw Dean standing before me wearing just his boxer shorts, I noticed the bulge in between his legs, I liked where this was going.

"Is it ok for me to join you?" he huskily asked me.

I just gave him a cheeky smile; I touched my breasts then tweaked my nipples. I heard him let out a small groan as I obviously hadn't given him an answer to his question.

"Please don't tease me." He pleaded, it felt good that I was the one in control of this moment. I walked over to him dripping wet feeling the cold air touch my warm skin. I placed my right hand onto his chest, Dean flinched with delight at my touch. I placed my left hand onto his aroused penis and stroked it gently over the top of his boxers.

"Oh, you sexy bitch."

He couldn't resist me any longer, moving in to kiss me passionately. Dean removed his now wet boxers and flung them out the way. His lips moved to my neck, then down to my breasts, licking my nipples. I always loved him doing that to my nipples. Then his lips moved lower and lower towards my thighs, licking his way to my pussy. I stroked my fingers through his wet hair whilst I enjoyed the pleasure he was doing to my lady area, sucking my clit. I let out a little groan as I climaxed into his mouth. He stood up, turned me round so my back was to him, moving his fingers through my now wet pussy then up to my breasts tweaking my nipples. He inserted his aroused penis inside of me, thrusting whilst holding my breasts. The hot water still pouring over us. I knew how much he wanted me as it didn't take him too long to cum. He held me gently after his orgasm still kissing my neck.

"I'm still so sorry after the way I've treated you." He whispered into my ear.

"Let's save all the apologies for now and just embrace this moment. I've got to be interrogated yet by your colleagues."

"I will be close by, if it gets too much, I promise I will stop it."

"Thank you. "

*****

This is where I ended up, at the ministry of defence in a secluded location, I'd gone over with the two agents the last six months of my life working in Amsterdam. I told them all I knew about Chris and that I had nothing to do with the acts of terrorism he was plotting. The funding of drugs was just a fragment of his crimes he would be prosecuted for. I was feeling like a criminal now being interrogated, I still hadn't fully mourned over Sophie, I knew Maria was being question in the room next door. Chris had promised me that if things got too difficult then he would intervene however I know there is limitations to his job about being too involved on a mission.

"Are you sure you've told us everything?"

I was getting bored now of being asked the same question over and over again, I was innocent in all of this, I just rolled my eyes at the two agents.

"Please answer the answer."

"Yes, I've told you everything I know and what I've been through. Am I free to go?"

The door opened and Dean entered, I was relieved to see him.

"Boss says she can go." He winked at me.

I let out a huge sigh of relief, I leapt up from off the chair and headed towards Dean then onto the exit.

"Lucy can you just follow me into here?" Dean ushered me into another nearby secluded room, I followed him. As I entered the next room there was another agent sat behind a desk, this chap had a much more friendly appearance about him compared to the other agents I'd seen.

"Hello Lucy, I'm Dean's superior officer, please take a seat."

I sat down on the comfy seat before his desk. In front of him looked to be a small case file, he opened it up.

"I want you to know that I've had an agent track down Jack, we have him in custody. I promise you he won't get away with what he did to your cousin. Please accept my deepest condolences on the loss of Sophie. But I want you to know it is in hand and I will find a way to charge him for her death."

I collapsed back into the chair, I know this will never bring back Sophie but to have the guy who caused all of this to her be charged with her death, this was a huge relief for me. It was as though a rock had been lifted off me.

"Thank you, thank you," Was all I could say whilst trying to hold back the tears.

"You're welcome, I do want you to know as well, we've found you accommodation to stay as well as sourced all your earnings from Amsterdam into your bank account. Everything is all in hand. Dean will take you to your new home now. You are free to go."

Through my tears I smiled at Dean's superior officer, my life back in England was looking for a promising start.

Epilogue: Lucy

It's been two weeks since I landed back in England, I've settled nicely into my new home, it isn't too far away from where Dean is based at for the Ministry Of Defence, so I get to see him most evenings. He's been trying to make amends for everything and has proposed to me, of course I said yes as he did save me from Chris and working at the Red Light District. For now, I'm enjoying some well needed rest as well as living under the witness protection programme in case any of Chris' henchmen tracks me down. Maria is living next door to me, I'm so grateful to have her in my life still. I know she is seeing Tye but taking things at a steady pace, he seems to be besotted towards her which is refreshing to see. I'm awaiting Jack's trial dates to come through, but he has admitted to everything, even possessing the drug that ended Sophie's life. Although he can't be trialled for her death but to know he is being trialled for raping her again and in possessions of the drug, that is more than what I could ask for to get justice for Sophie.

The End

Acknowledgments

Johnathan Spink. Thank you for introducing to me, the beautiful city of Amsterdam, if we hadn't visited there then this story would never have happened.

Globe Writers. Thank you for your continued support, you've all helped me along my writing journey.

Spellbound Books. Thank you, Sumaira and Nicky, I look forward to working with you both on my next book.

Ants Ambridge. Thank you on your help, support and guidance with each of my books. Without you they wouldn't be out there in the world today.

A special thank you to my beta readers Elizabeth Morse and June Vernau, I'm so grateful to both of you for putting in the time to reading my manuscript of Red Light Romance, along with feedback for this book.

A special mention to Swanwick Writers Summer School, I look forward to attending my third year August 2024.

Other Books by
Gemma Owen-Kendall

Girl In the Red Coat

Innocent Times

A Fallen Star

Stars and Wishes

Collaborations:

Christmas Gifts

Tales From Lockdown

Halloween Screams

A New World

Monday At Six

Fish & Freaks

This book is copyright of the author.

Printed in Great Britain
by Amazon